A FOREVER HOME FOR TIGER

Tiger suddenly put both paws on
the edge of the bowl and tipped
over. Water cascaded over the
or and the ball floated out with
Tiger gave chase, splashing
ough the water and leaving
ail of paw prints.

HAVE YOU READ?

A FOREVER HOME FOR **TILLY**

A FOREVER HOME FOR **PIP**

A FOREVER HOME FOR **LUNA**

A FOREVER HOME FOR **FLUFFY**

A FOREVER HOME FOR **BELLA**

A FOREVER HOME FOR TIGER

LINDA CHAPMAN

Illustrated By
Sophy Williams

nosy
crow

First published in the UK in 2021 by Nosy Crow Ltd
The Crow's Nest, 14 Baden Place
Crosby Row, London SE1 1YW

Nosy Crow and associated logos are trademarks and/or
registered trademarks of Nosy Crow Ltd.

Text copyright © Linda Chapman and Julie Sykes, 2021
Illustrations © Sophy Williams, 2021

The right of Linda Chapman, Julie Sykes and Sophy Williams
to be identified as the authors and illustrator respectively of this
work has been asserted by them in accordance with the Copyright,
Designs and Patents Act 1988.

ISBN: 978 1 78800 971 3

A CIP catalogue record for this book will be available from the British Library.

Printed and bound in Great Britain by Clays Ltd, Elcograf S.p.A.

Papers used by Nosy Crow are made from
wood grown in sustainable forests.

MIX
Paper from
responsible sources
FSC® C018072

1 3 5 7 9 10 8 6 4 2

www.nosycrow.com

To Mabel Knight, for when you are older.

CHAPTER 1

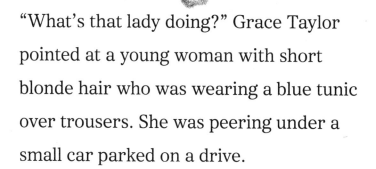

"What's that lady doing?" Grace Taylor
pointed at a young woman with short
blonde hair who was wearing a blue tunic
over trousers. She was peering under a
small car parked on a drive.

"It looks like she's lost something," said

    1

Jack.

It was a warm Friday afternoon in September and twins Grace and Jack were on their way home from school.

"Here, Tiger," the woman coaxed. "Please come out."

Grace crouched down. She could just see a tiny cat hiding under the car. "It's a kitten! Let's see if she needs a hand."

Grace hurried up the drive with Jack following. "Do you need help getting your kitten out?"

A look of relief crossed the young woman's face. "Thanks. I'm a care worker. I'm visiting Mrs Brownlee who lives here, but just as I opened my car door, my kitten jumped out." She smiled. "I'm Emma, by the way, and this is Tiger."

The twins smiled back. "I'm Grace and this is Jack," said Grace. She peered under the car. The kitten, a silver tabby with grey and white stripes, a fluffy white chest and blue eyes, stared back.

"You must have got a shock when Tiger jumped out of the car with you," Jack said.

Emma sighed. "Not really – it's not the first time it's happened. Tiger doesn't like being left alone in the house so he tries to sneak into the car when I'm putting my things inside. It's becoming quite a problem." She checked her watch. "Oh dear, I'm going to be late if he doesn't come out soon."

Jack got a little rubber ball out of his bag. "Let's try rolling this past him and see if he'll chase it out." He hurried to the other side of the car. "Ready, Grace?"

"Ready!" said Grace.

Jack rolled the ball and Tiger watched it. As it passed his paws he pounced and bounded after it on to the drive.

"Got you!" Grace scooped him up.

"Thank you!" cried Emma.

"Stop wriggling," Grace giggled as Tiger meowed and struggled in her arms. "I'm not going to hurt you. He's gorgeous," she told Emma.

"He's also a bundle of trouble." Emma sighed as she stroked Tiger's fluffy head. "I don't know what to do with him now. I don't want to leave him in the car but I can't take him into Mrs Brownlee's."

"We'll look after him," offered Jack. "We only live five minutes away. Our mum has a doggy day care business called Top Dog. You can come round to get him when you finish work."

Emma's face lit up. "Top Dog? My friend's poodle Lolly goes there. It would

   5

be really kind of you to kitten-sit. Are you sure your mum won't mind?"

"She'll be fine," said Grace, thrilled at the thought of having some time with such a cute kitten. "Jack and I often look after animals."

"We run an animal rehoming business called Forever Homes," Jack explained. He took one of their home-made business cards out of his school bag and handed it to Emma. "Here's our address."

Emma studied the card, her forehead crinkling. "An animal rehoming business?"

"We find new homes for dogs and cats when their owners can't keep them any more," said Jack.

"Perfect forever homes," said Grace happily.

"Do ... do you think you could help me find Tiger a new home?" asked Emma slowly.

Excitement rushed through Grace. "I bet we could!"

"If you're sure you want him rehomed?" said Jack, more cautiously.

Emma sighed. "I think it would be for the best. I love Tiger to bits but he needs an owner who isn't out at work all day; someone to keep him out of mischief."

"There's bound to be an owner out there who will suit him perfectly," said Grace, tickling Tiger under his chin. He purred so loudly, his whole body shook.

"You could come round when you've finished work and sign the paperwork," said Jack.

"OK. I'll also bring his vaccination certificate and the rest of his kitten food." Emma gave Tiger a sad smile. "I hate saying goodbye but I'm sure this is the right thing for Tiger."

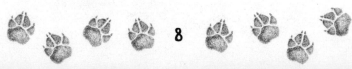

"We promise we'll look after him really well," Grace told her.

Jack nodded firmly. "And we'll only rehome him when we find the absolutely perfect forever home!"

Grace and Jack took turns carrying Tiger back to their house. Luckily it wasn't far because he kept wriggling and at one point almost climbed over Grace's shoulder!

"He's definitely lively!" she gasped as she gently untangled his claws from her coat.

Tiger meowed.

"We'll have to run a personality test on him when we get home," said Jack. The twins ran a personality test on every new animal. It helped them work out exactly what kind of owner the animal needed.

"I'm so happy we've got a new cat to look after," said Grace. "I love kittens!"

"And, best of all, it's the weekend, which means we'll have lots of time to get to know him," said Jack.

They reached their house, an old red-brick Victorian villa, and went through a gate into the small courtyard at the side of the house. Opposite the house there was a modern building where their mum ran Top Dog. Hearing the gate opening, she came to the door.

"Hi, you two, how was—" Mrs Taylor broke off in surprise. "A kitten!"

"Yes, he's called Tiger," said Grace. She and Jack quickly explained everything that had happened.

"His owner is coming round later to sign

the paperwork," Jack finished.

Mum smiled and tickled Tiger's head. "He's absolutely gorgeous! I can't imagine you'll struggle to find a cutie like him a home."

"We're going to take him to the shed and run a personality test," said Jack. "Come on, Grace."

Mum went back inside Top Dog and the twins set off to their office shed. Suddenly there was a yell from inside the house, followed by a loud crash.

Grace and Jack stared at each other and then, together, they sprinted to the door.

CHAPTER 2

Jack pulled the door open and coughed as a cloud of smoke billowed out. Grace shielded Tiger from it with her hand.

"Oh, wow," she said, staring into the family's large kitchen. "Ollie! What have you been doing?"

    12

Ollie, the twins' seventeen-year-old brother, was standing by the cooker, and Tiny, the family's big white dog, was hiding under the wooden table. Dirty bowls and wooden spoons covered every surface and a half-dismantled food mixer was dripping raw cake mixture on to the dresser. Every surface was coated with a dusting of flour and there was an upturned tray of burnt cupcakes on the floor.

Jack's eyebrows rose. "Ollie, have you been *baking*?"

Ollie looked ruefully at the cakes on the floor. "I was trying to bake some cakes for the next rehearsal." Ollie was in a band with some friends from his sixth-form college. "But I guess we can't eat them now."

"Probably just as well," said Grace, looking at the blackened cakes.

Ollie noticed Tiger in her arms. "Hey, that's a cute kitten!" he said, walking over and stroking Tiger, who rubbed his cheek against Ollie's hand. Both Ollie and Amelia, the twins' thirteen-year-old sister, loved animals, although they weren't quite as animal-crazy as Grace and Jack. "What's its name?"

"Tiger," said Grace. "We've got him in for rehoming."

She put Tiger on the floor. The kitten padded over to the cakes and sniffed at them. His nose wrinkled and with a delicate shake of his paw, he turned away. "Even Tiger doesn't like the look of your cakes!" Grace said with a giggle.

   **14**

"I hadn't realised baking was so hard," sighed Ollie as Tiny gave a little woof from under the table and thumped his tail. Tiger boldly walked over to say hello to the big dog. "I baked a few times with Auntie Meg when I was younger and she made it seem easy!"

Auntie Meg was their mum's sister. She lived on a houseboat called the *Happy Otter*. She made delicious cakes and had opened up a tea shop on her boat. She was never in one place for more than a few days, moving around the country on the canal network. She was loud and cheerful and she always forgot their birthdays but they all adored her and her cakes!

"Auntie Meg's red velvet cake, yum!" said Jack longingly.

"Chocolate brownies and rocky road cookies," sighed Grace.

Ollie groaned. "Stop it! My mouth's watering!"

Grace looked round at the mess. "So what made you decide to bake today?"

Ollie shrugged. "I just thought it would be a..." He cleared his throat. "A nice way to welcome the band's new singer." His cheeks turned slightly pink.

Grace's eyes widened as she noticed the

blush. "Wait a sec. The new singer's a girl called Ellie, isn't she? Ollie, are you trying to impress her?"

Ollie's face turned beetroot red. "No, no, of course I'm not!"

Grace nudged Jack. "Ollie's in lurv!" she grinned.

Jack sniggered. "Ollie and Ella sitting in a tree," he chanted. "K ... I ... S ... S ... I—" He broke off to dodge away as Ollie grabbed a sticky spoon from the side and tried to swat him with it.

"Where's Tiger?" Grace asked suddenly. "He was here just a second ago."

"He must have gone exploring!" Jack went to the open door that led to the hall. "Tiger? Here, puss!"

Grace and Jack searched the hall, the

lounge and the study but Tiger was nowhere to be seen.

"Maybe he went upstairs?" Grace ran up the stairs with Jack following. They could hear Amelia in the bathroom laughing with her best friend Freya, and there was the sound of water running.

"He's so cute!" they heard Freya exclaim.

"Aw! Look at his little tongue!" said Amelia.

The twins hurried to the bathroom.

Amelia and Freya were inside, their school bags at their feet. They were watching Tiger as he balanced on the edge of the sink. His tail was twitching as he lapped water straight from the gushing tap with his little pink tongue.

   18

"Found him!" Jack said to Grace.

"Is he another Forever Homes kitten?" asked Amelia, pushing her long hair back behind her ears.

Grace nodded and explained how they had come to be looking after him.

"He's really funny," said Freya as Tiger started batting the stream of water with one paw. "We were going into Amelia's

room when we saw him run in here. He
jumped on the sink and started nudging
the tap with his nose."

"He wanted a drink and knew water
came out of the tap," said Amelia. "Clever
kitty."

"That's probably enough now though,"
said Jack, turning the tap off.

"Prrip!" squeaked Tiger indignantly. He
shook his whiskers and then started to
walk round the basin edge. He wobbled
and Jack caught him.

"Meow!" Tiger squirmed in his arms.

"You're coming with me and Grace
now," said Jack. "No more exploring."

"Can I have a quick cuddle first?" asked
Freya eagerly.

Jack handed him over. Freya held him

   20

close. "I love kittens!" she sighed.

"You don't want to adopt him, do you?" Grace asked hopefully. She liked Freya.

"I'd love to but Mum's allergic to cats. I'll ask around though." Tiger started to struggle and Freya put him down. "Do you just rehome kittens and puppies or do you rehome older animals too?"

"We usually end up with kittens and puppies but we'll rehome any cat or dog," said Jack, pushing the door shut with his foot so Tiger couldn't go off exploring again.

"Really?" Freya's eyes lit up. "Can you help my auntie? She's moving to America and she needs to find a new home for Connie, her cocker spaniel. Connie's ten and my auntie doesn't think she should take her to America because the flight is really long and she's renting a city flat. She's trying to find Connie a new home but no luck so far."

"We'd love to help—" Grace started but Jack cut in.

"But we can't. Mum and Dad only let us take in one animal at a time." He gave Grace a firm look.

Grace sighed, knowing Jack was right. Their parents were very supportive of Forever Homes but they were also very strict about the twins only taking on one animal at a time.

"No worries!" said Freya. "My auntie's not moving quite yet. There's still time to find Connie a good home."

"If we find a new owner for Tiger really quickly then we might be able to help with Connie," said Grace.

"That would be great!" said Freya, smiling.

    23

"Come on, Frey, let's go to my room," said Amelia.

Freya picked up her school bag and then squealed as the side of it suddenly moved. "What's in my..."

They all burst out laughing as Tiger poked his head out of the bag's opening. "Meow!" he said, looking delighted to be the centre of attention.

"Oh, Tiger!" Jack said as Freya took him out and handed him to Grace. "Emma was right. You're a bundle of trouble."

"A super-cute bundle," said Grace, kissing the top of Tiger's fluffy head.

CHAPTER 3

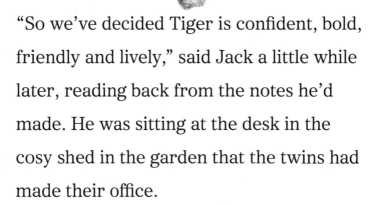

"So we've decided Tiger is confident, bold, friendly and lively," said Jack a little while later, reading back from the notes he'd made. He was sitting at the desk in the cosy shed in the garden that the twins had made their office.

   25

On one wall hung a pinboard with photos of animals they had rehomed, and the other walls were decorated with pet pictures drawn by Grace. There was a rug on the floor and several boxes of dog and cat toys. On the desk there were some jars of treats, and paperwork including questionnaires for possible owners to fill in, business cards and a form for owners to sign when they brought their animal in for rehoming.

"Have you written down that he likes to play?" said Grace, flicking a fluffy cat toy on a stick from side to side and watching Tiger pounce on it. As part of the personality test, she and Jack checked whether the animal liked to play with toys. They also made notes on how friendly

the animal was, and watched to see how
bold they were. Tiger had investigated
all corners of the shed and he certainly
seemed to like being cuddled, so he'd been
given a tick in the boxes marked "bold"
and "friendly".

"Yes, and that he likes company," said Jack. "He needs a home where he isn't left on his own for too long."

"He'd be perfect for a big family," said Grace, "with lots of people to play with him."

"He wasn't scared of Tiny," said Jack, making another note. "Which means he could go to a home with dogs." He put his pen down. "OK, we're done with the testing." He got up and went to stroke Tiger.

"We could make some posters about him tonight and put them in the usual places," said Grace, listing them on her fingers. "The vet's, the newsagent's, the post office and at school."

"Good plan." Jack stroked a hand down

   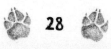

Tiger's back. The kitten purred. "We'll find him a perfect home soon, I'm sure!"

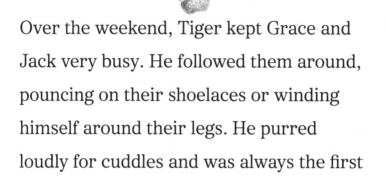

Over the weekend, Tiger kept Grace and Jack very busy. He followed them around, pouncing on their shoelaces or winding himself around their legs. He purred loudly for cuddles and was always the first through an open door. The twins soon found out that if they left him alone for any length of time he would get into all sorts of mischief.

On Saturday morning, after the twins came back from putting up some posters about Tiger, they found that he had walked along the kitchen dresser knocking bills, dog leads and a packet of rice on to the floor. He had then gone into the

    29

downstairs bathroom and fallen asleep in the sink!

"Oh, Tiger," Jack sighed as he started to sweep up the grains of rice. "You really can't be left alone for a second!"

"Meow!" Tiger agreed from Grace's arms.

She put him down and he trotted over to Tiny. He started climbing on to Tiny's head while the big dog tried to snooze.

"Oh, no you don't!" Grace ignored Tiger's sharp mew of protest as she lifted him up. "Tiny's having a rest. Here, play with this."

She took a ball from the side and rolled it along the floor. Tiger pounced, knocking the ball into the air. It splashed down into Tiny's water bowl. Grace went to get it out – cats weren't usually keen on water – but before she got there, Tiger had bounded over and was trying to fish the ball out with his paws.

"Tiger!" Grace exclaimed as Tiger suddenly put both paws on the edge of the bowl and tipped it over. Water cascaded over the floor and the ball floated out with it. Tiger gave chase, splashing through the water and spreading it further round the kitchen in a trail of watery paw prints.

"He really seems to like water," said
Grace to Jack. "We should add that to
his personality test. He's a very unusual
kitten."

Just then Ollie came in, singing loudly.
Tiger ran under his feet and Ollie hopped

to avoid standing on him but as he landed,
his feet slipped on the rice and water
and his arms spun frantically. "Oof!" he
exclaimed as he landed on his bottom.

"All the grace of a ballerina. Not!" said
Jack with a grin.

Grace giggled as Ollie scrambled to his feet, unhurt. "You look like you've had an accident!"

Ollie twisted round to look at the damp seat of his jeans and groaned. "I'm going to have to get changed now. That kitten's a menace!" he exclaimed, stomping out of the room.

"Oh, Tiger," said Grace, picking the kitten up and kissing his nose. "What are we going to do with you?"

Jack grabbed some cloths from under the sink and mopped up the water. "Find him a home with someone who has a ton of energy for playing and who doesn't mind cleaning up a mess. I hope someone sees our posters and gets in touch soon!"

Although the twins had a few phone calls that night and on Sunday from people who had seen the posters about Tiger, no one who rang was suitable.

"I'm sorry," Grace told the fourth caller, a lady called Sue, "but Tiger really needs a home where he isn't alone for long periods of time."

She put the phone down.

"No good?" said Jack.

Grace shook her head. "She sounded

really nice but she works full time—" She broke off as the phone rang again.

Jack picked it up. "Hello," he said politely. His face broke into a grin. "Auntie Meg! Hi! We're all fine. Mum? Yes, she's here. I'll go and find her."

He took the phone into the lounge, chatting to their auntie. He came back a few minutes later.

"Where's Auntie Meg now?" asked Grace. "Did she say?"

"Not too far from here," said Jack.

"Brilliant!" said Grace. "Is she coming to see us?"

Mum came in, still talking on the phone. "A sleepover on the *Happy Otter*?" she said, catching Grace's and Jack's eyes. "Yes, I'm sure the twins would love that. I'll just ask. You two, Auntie Meg wants to know if you'd like to stay the night with her this coming Friday?"

"Definitely!" Grace and Jack exclaimed together. They loved staying on their aunt's busy canal boat and tea room. She let them help serve the customers, and in the evening they got to eat any leftovers. They were also allowed to stay up late and even eat cake for breakfast!

Mum grinned. "I imagine you heard that, Meg? That's a definite yes please. It's good timing. Mike and I are going out to dinner that night so we won't have to ask Ollie to babysit."

"Yay!" said Grace when Mum ended the call. "A sleepover with Auntie Meg!"

"Hang on, what about Tiger?" Jack said suddenly. "We can't leave him on his own all evening."

"Amelia might look after him," suggested Grace.

"She's out at Freya's," said Mum. "But I bet if you bribe Ollie with some of Auntie Meg's cakes, he'll agree to stay in."

"Stay in when?" Ollie asked, coming into the kitchen.

"On Friday night," said Grace. "To kitten-sit."

Mum explained.

   38

"We'll bring you cake back if you look after Tiger," offered Jack.

"OK," said Ollie with a shrug. "I'll kitten-sit." He picked Tiger up from the floor. "Just no more tripping me up," he said sternly to the little kitten.

Tiger's blue eyes sparkled and he purred.

CHAPTER 4

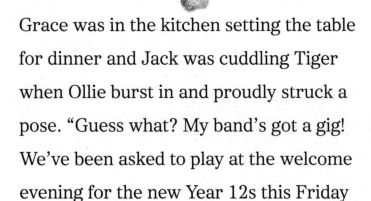

Grace was in the kitchen setting the table for dinner and Jack was cuddling Tiger when Ollie burst in and proudly struck a pose. "Guess what? My band's got a gig! We've been asked to play at the welcome evening for the new Year 12s this Friday

evening!"

"That's great news," said Dad, who was stirring a pan of gravy.

Amelia glanced round from the sink with a smirk. "Ooh, Ollie. I'd better get your autograph before your band make it REALLY big," she teased. "This Friday college, next stop Wembley."

Ollie huffed. "You can laugh all you want but this is how a lot of the big bands started."

"Wait!" said Jack, realising something. "You can't play on Friday. You promised to look after Tiger for us."

Ollie put his finger to his cheek and tilted his head as if he was thinking. "Hmm ... let me see. First ever gig or kitten-sitting? That's a tough one... Sorry, guys, you'll have to find someone else to look after the kitten."

"Ollie! That's not fair!" Grace said crossly.

"You did promise," Jack reminded him.

"Dad!" Grace appealed. "Make him look after Tiger!"

"No way!" protested Ollie.

Dad held his hands up. "Whoa, everyone! I'm sure we can sort this out." He thought for a moment. "How about you take Tiger with you? Meg loves cats and I think that between you all, you can keep him out of trouble on the boat."

"Ringing her now!" gasped Grace, snatching the phone from the table.

A few minutes later, after a short conversation, Grace came off the phone, her face triumphant. "Auntie Meg said yes!" she burst out.

Ollie whooped and, punching the air, he hurried out of the room.

Grace went on. "Auntie Meg's exact words were '*Tiger sounds a hoot!*' She says she's very happy for him to come on board and can't wait to meet him." She noticed Jack was frowning. "What is it? I thought you'd be pleased."

"Tiger on a canal boat?" said Jack. "Water and cats? It's not the best combination. What if he hates it or gets into trouble?"

"You know Tiger's not like most cats – he loves water," said Grace. "And Dad's right – between us we can keep an eye on him."

"OK," said Jack slowly. "But we'll have to be very careful."

"We will," promised Grace.

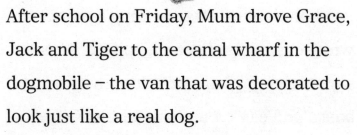

After school on Friday, Mum drove Grace, Jack and Tiger to the canal wharf in the dogmobile – the van that was decorated to look just like a real dog.

"There's the *Happy Otter*, and there's Auntie Meg!" exclaimed Grace.

There were several boats moored at the wharf, but the *Happy Otter* was easy to spot as it was the most colourful. It was bright red, green and yellow, and painted with tiny pictures of otters playing together. The roof was like a floating garden. It was packed with pots of colourful flowers, and rainbow-coloured bunting was strung between them.

Auntie Meg had stuck a banner on a pole beside the towpath, advertising the Happy Otter Teashop. It had her trademark symbol of a cute otter holding a pink and white cupcake between its paws. To the side of the towpath, on a stretch of grass, were several fold-up tables, each with two

chairs. They were full of customers – some
of them already had tea in spotted teapots,
and matching mugs and big plates of cake.

"Auntie Meg looks busy," said Grace,
having noticed their auntie bustling round

between the tables, a pencil tucked into
her short pink hair and an apron over her
jeans and biker boots.

Jack lifted Tiger's travel basket out of
the van and reached back in for their bags.

    47

"Tell Meg I'll stop for a proper catch-up when I come and collect you," said Mum. "She looks too busy now."

Auntie Meg waved cheerfully as Grace and Jack hurried over. She wasn't the type of auntie who hugged much. Instead, she greeted them with high-fives. "Hey there, you terrible twins!" she exclaimed. "And this must be Tiger. Let me have a look."

She peered inside the basket. Grace saw her catch her breath.

"Well, well." Auntie Meg's voice became unusually soft. "Aren't you a beauty?" Tiger mewed and Auntie Meg chuckled. "Yes, and you know it, don't you?" She straightened up and grinned at Grace and Jack. "You can let him out when you're inside the boat. I bet my customers will

   48

love him!"

Feeling very important, Grace carried Tiger past the tables and over the tiny gangplank to board the *Happy Otter*. She ducked to go through the low door and carefully went down the two steps into the tea room. The *Happy Otter* was divided into three cabins. The first was the biggest, with a galley kitchen along one side and four tables full of chatting customers along the other. The walls were hung with polka-dot bunting and there were more pictures of otters. Shelves were stacked with teapots, cups and plates, and a cuddly otter had pride of place on the top shelf.

The two further cabins were bedrooms, both sharing a teensy bathroom with a

toilet and shower. Jack quickly put their bag in the smaller cabin with the bunk beds. There were two *Happy Otter* aprons on the lower bunk. He and Grace put them on and then Grace let Tiger out. He strutted into the main cabin with his tail held high. His nose twitched as he took in his new surroundings then confidently he went round the tables, sniffing the people and rubbing his head against their legs to say hello.

There was a chorus of delighted exclamations from the customers.

"What a gorgeous kitten!"

"He's adorable!"

"Meg? Is this your kitten?" asked one lady as Auntie Meg came in with a tray full of empty plates.

"Nope," Auntie Meg said. "No pets for me – not living on a boat and travelling round as much as I do. Pity, he's a gem." She smiled at Grace and Jack. "Come on, you two, get cracking. There are some more dirty plates outside and table three needs two teacakes and a fresh pot of tea."

Grace and Jack washed their hands and hurried to help. Soon they were busy taking people their food and clearing tables. Grace had just taken a tray of fresh scones, jam and clotted cream to an elderly lady who was sitting alone when she glanced up. Tiger was walking confidently along the roof of the houseboat!

"Tiger!" Grace gasped.

The lady followed her gaze. "Is that your kitten?"

"Yes!" Grace gulped as Tiger reached the edge of the roof and peered curiously down at the canal water below. Grace watched in alarm as he wobbled precariously.

"Oh no!" she gasped. "He's going to fall!"

    53

CHAPTER 5

Abandoning the customer, Grace ran towards the boat, her heart thumping as Tiger swayed but then, in one fluid movement, he twisted round and jumped down, landing neatly on the gangplank. He ran across it. Grace took a shaky

breath. Phew! For a moment, she had been
sure he was going to end up in the canal!

Jack looked out of the main cabin. "Have
you seen Tiger?"

"He's here," said Grace, pointing to
where Tiger was introducing himself to
the customers. One elderly gentleman sat
rigid, watching Tiger. The kitten singled
him out and, reaching a paw up, he
jumped on to the man's lap.

The man caught his breath. "Um..." He
looked around desperately. "I don't really
like cats," he said, holding his hands in the
air.

Both Grace and Jack hurried to rescue
him but the lady Grace had been serving
reached the table first. "Oh, John, how
can you not like this lovely little kitten?"

She scooped Tiger up from the man's lap. "Leave grumpy Uncle John alone and come to Auntie Barbara."

"I'm really sorry," Grace apologised to the elderly man. "Tiger was supposed to be inside the boat."

"He must have got out while we were busy," said Jack.

"You wanted to say hello to everyone out here, didn't you, little one?" cooed Barbara, gently rubbing Tiger's cheek. He purred. "Say hello to him, John," she said, holding the kitten out to the man. "Go on."

Cautiously, the elderly man stroked Tiger's head. The kitten nuzzled his hand encouragingly. A smile broke out on the man's wrinkled face. "He is rather sweet," he said gruffly.

Tiger purred.

Barbara turned to Grace and Jack. "I love cats – dogs too."

"Just like us," said Grace with a smile. "We love all animals!"

Barbara carried Tiger back to her table

   57

and sat down. "You're very lucky to have such a gorgeous kitten. I've been thinking about getting a cat since Skip, my Border terrier, died a few months ago. He was fifteen and such good company. How he loved his walks!" Her eyes misted over as she remembered, and she sighed. "I'd love another dog but I'm not sure I could cope with a lively young puppy."

The words burst from Grace. "Tiger's looking for a new home! Maybe you could have him!"

"Really?" In her surprise, Barbara stopped stroking Tiger for a second and he butted her hand impatiently.

Between them, Grace and Jack explained about Forever Homes.

"Would you really be interested in being

Tiger's new forever owner?" asked Grace
eagerly.

"We'd have to ask you some questions
first and visit your home to see if it was
suitable for a kitten," Jack put in quickly.

"I'm certainly interested," said Barbara.
"Ask away."

Grace's hopes grew as she and Jack
asked Barbara about her home. She told
them she was retired and lived alone apart
from when her teenage grandchildren
visited. She lived in a quiet street away
from a main road. She had a small, fenced
garden. She'd always had dogs and knew
how much time animals took up. She
sounded perfect and Tiger seemed to
really like her!

"You sound ideal," said Jack, looking at

Grace, who nodded hard. "We would just need to do a home visit though, if that's OK?"

"That's fine," said Barbara. "When can you come round?"

Grace ran inside and after telling Auntie Meg what was happening, she borrowed her mobile to ring Mum. Soon it was arranged. Mum would drive them to Barbara's house the following morning when she picked them up from the boat. If Barbara passed the home check, they would leave Tiger with her.

"I can't believe we've found Tiger a new home so quickly!" Grace said. The tea shop was closed and the three of them were sitting inside at a table. Tiger was

curled up on Auntie Meg's lap. The twins were drinking hot chocolate topped with whipped cream, chocolate shavings and marshmallows, from massive mugs.

"It's brilliant!" said Jack. "If Barbara's house is as she says, then she'll be perfect."

"I feel very jealous of Barbara!" Auntie Meg stroked Tiger, who was purring loudly. "If she hadn't wanted him, I was thinking of offering myself. He's my kind of cat. Different," she added approvingly. "He doesn't seem bothered by the water and he's so friendly. He would have made an excellent canal-boat cat."

"Auntie Meg! You didn't tell us you were looking for a cat!" Grace said, swapping dismayed looks with Jack. Barbara was great but if they'd known their aunt wanted a kitten, they would definitely have offered Tiger to her first.

"I wasn't," their aunt replied. "I didn't

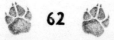

think it fair to have an animal with the life I have. But this little guy has stolen my heart. He's so at home here and the customers loved him." A wistful look crossed her face. "It would have been good to have the company – it does get a bit lonely on the boat sometimes." She gave her head a rueful shake. "But I'm sure Barbara will give him a great home."

"Auntie Meg, I want you to have him!" Grace burst out.

Jack nodded. "Tiger would love living on a boat!"

Hope fluttered in Grace's chest. "Couldn't we just tell Barbara that we've found him another home?"

"Absolutely not!" Auntie Meg said firmly, getting up. "That would be very unkind.

Barbara's one of the nicest people you could meet and you've already offered Tiger to her. I shouldn't have said anything. Anyway, my customers keep me company and my baking keeps me busy. I don't need a cat. Now, drink up and I'll make some bacon sarnies."

She settled Tiger back on the chair where she'd been sitting and moved to the stove. Tiger curled up with his nose resting on his tail and fell asleep.

"Jack, isn't there anything we can do?" Grace whispered, watching her aunt cook. "The *Happy Otter* would be a perfect home for Tiger. He'd have lots of company and he loves water and travelling! I really want Auntie Meg to have him."

"I know," said Jack sadly. "But she's right. We can't tell Barbara we've changed our minds. It would be really mean."

Grace bit her lip. If only there was something they could do!

CHAPTER 6

The following morning, Mum arrived
to pick up Grace and Jack. Auntie Meg
gave Tiger a last cuddle. "Bye, Tiger,"
she murmured into his soft fur. "Be
happy." Brushing quickly at her eyes, she
handed him to Jack, who put him into his

travelling basket. Then she hurried to get the boat ready to travel on.

Mum drove the twins to Barbara's house.

"Did you bring the new-owner forms with you for Barbara to fill in?" Jack asked her. He'd rung Mum the night before and asked if she would get the forms from the shed.

"Yes, here you go," Mum said, taking them out of her bag and giving them to him.

She waited in the van as they carried Tiger in his basket up to the front door.

Barbara greeted them with a broad smile and showed them around the house, finishing the tour in the cosy living room, which had doors that opened into the garden. "You can let him outside so he can have a look around. I've put some drinking water out there in Skip's old water bowl," she said.

They all went outside. Jack unfastened the carrier.

"Hello, kitty." Barbara bent to greet Tiger as he walked inquisitively out of the carrier. He wound himself around her legs, rubbing his head against her outstretched hand.

Grace felt torn. She desperately wanted Auntie Meg to be his new owner but Barbara was clearly smitten and it was clear that Tiger liked her back. *If only we had two Tigers*, she thought longingly.

"So have I passed the home test?" Barbara asked, straightening up.

Jack nodded. "We just need you to fill in a form with your details and sign it to say that you'll take care of Tiger."

"We'd better go inside. I'll need my glasses," said Barbara.

"Should we bring Tiger in?" asked Grace.

"He can have a little explore. All the plants out here are safe for cats," said Barbara.

They went into the lounge. Barbara put on her reading glasses and sat in a chair with the paperwork balanced on her knee. She read slowly and carefully then picked up her pen to sign. Grace let out a sigh. This was it then. She was really happy for Tiger but—

A high-pitched yowl broke into her

thoughts. Barbara leapt up, scattering papers everywhere.

"Cat fight!" she cried, rushing outside.

Grace and Jack followed quickly. A huge black cat with a torn ear was circling Tiger. His tail twitched furiously. Tiger was crouched low to the ground. Before anyone could stop him, the black cat threw himself at Tiger.

   70

Tiger sprang back. He looked so tiny
next to the black cat, but he hissed, his
coat fluffing out. The black cat leapt at
him again, forcing him to the ground and
rolling him over. Bravely, Tiger batted him
with a paw but the black cat was bigger
and stronger. Both cats yowled and hissed.

"Stop that!" said Grace, rushing across
the grass.

"Grace, wait! You'll get scratched." Jack
grabbed the bowl of water and threw it
at the cats. The black cat let Tiger go.
With a hiss, he sprang on to the fence and
disappeared into the neighbour's garden.
Tiger shook his paws, delicately spraying
water, then he swaggered over to Jack and
headbutted his leg as if to say thank you.

Grace scooped Tiger up and kissed him.

"You brave little thing! I thought you were toast!"

"Is he OK?" asked Barbara anxiously.

"He's fine, apart from a tiny scratch on his nose," said Jack, checking Tiger over.

"I'm so sorry!" Barbara said, stroking Tiger. "I should have remembered Bruiser, my next-door neighbour's cat. He never came in my garden when Skip was alive. Dearie me, I feel awful, but I don't think I can offer Tiger a home after all. It wouldn't be safe for him."

Jack nodded slowly. "Bruiser does change things," he said, glancing at Grace.

Grace nodded too, excitement flaring inside her. If Barbara couldn't have Tiger, then maybe Auntie Meg could! Seeing Barbara's disappointed face, she felt bad.

Poor Barbara. If only there was something they could do. Her eyes fell on the dog's water bowl. "Maybe you could adopt an older dog instead of a puppy—" She broke off with a gasp as an idea burst like a firework into her mind. "Jack! Freya's aunt!"

Jack's eyes widened as he realised what she was thinking. "The one who's moving abroad! It's perfect!" He swung round to Barbara. "Our friend's aunt has a ten-year-old cocker spaniel called Connie who needs a good home."

"She's moving to America and can't take the dog with her," Grace added.

"A cocker spaniel?" said Barbara. "I love cockers – I had a black one when I was growing up." Her face lit up with a smile.

"I'd be very interested in giving Connie a home. Will you put me in touch with her owner?"

"We'll find out her number as soon as we get home and give you a ring," promised Jack.

"But first we've got something else to do!" said Grace. She ran to the French windows, clutching Tiger. "Jack, bring the travel basket! We need to get to the canal before Auntie Meg leaves. Hurry!"

CHAPTER 7

The twins threw themselves into the van.

"What's going on?" their mum asked in surprise.

"Drive, Mum, please!" gasped Grace as Jack helped her put Tiger into his travel basket.

     75

"We need to get to Auntie Meg before she leaves," said Jack. He saw his mum's astonished face. "We'll explain as we go. Please drive, Mum!"

As Mum drove, the story tumbled out of the twins. "Auntie Meg's boat will be the perfect home for Tiger!" said Grace.

"If we can get there in time," said Jack anxiously.

"Ring Meg and tell her to wait," said Mum. "My phone's in my bag."

Grace dialled Auntie Meg's number. Jack held up crossed fingers.

Grace's face fell. "It's gone to voicemail!" she cried.

"It doesn't mean she's left yet," said Mum, her face setting into a determined frown as she manoeuvred the van through

 76

the traffic.

Grace willed her mother to go faster while Jack stared out of the window, his eyes fixed on the road. The drive to the canal seemed to take forever but at last they pulled into the car park at the canal wharf. Grace took Tiger out of his basket. "It'll be quicker to carry him!"

Clutching him to her chest, she followed Jack as he sprinted ahead. "The *Happy Otter*!" he shouted. "Look! It's just leaving!"

Grace saw her aunt's boat slowly cruising past the other boats tied to the bank.

"Auntie Meg, wait!" she shouted.

Jack joined in. "Auntie Meg!" he yelled.

People walking on the towpath turned

to stare, stepping out of their way as the twins raced after the boat.

"Auntie Meg, please stop!" Grace cried, her heart banging. She could see her aunt standing on the stern, her hand resting on the tiller. Two swans glided along in the middle of the canal. Grace felt suddenly hopeful as Auntie Meg slowed the *Happy Otter* and pushed the tiller to steer away from the birds.

"Auntie Meg!" she shrieked again at the top of her voice.

"Stop!" bellowed Jack.

Auntie Meg heard and glanced round. Her eyes widened with astonishment as she saw the twins. She brought the boat alongside the towpath and cut the engine. Holding on to the mooring rope,

she jumped ashore and tied the boat to a nearby tree.

"What's going on?" she asked as Grace and Jack ran up. "Did I forget something?"

"Yes," panted Grace, stopping to put Tiger down on the towpath. Tiger trotted towards Auntie Meg with a happy miaow.

"You forgot Tiger," said Jack with a grin.

Quickly the twins explained.

"He's yours if you still want him," said Jack.

"Do you?" Grace asked anxiously.

A smile lifted the corners of Auntie Meg's mouth. "Want him? You bet I do!"

"Just as well," said Jack, grinning and pointing at the open cabin door as Tiger disappeared inside. "He's already moved in!"

   80

Mum caught up with them. "Is everything sorted?" she panted. "Did you say yes?" she asked her sister.

Auntie Meg nodded. "Not that I had much choice with these two," she said with a chuckle.

"You are OK about it, aren't you?" Mum said anxiously.

"Absolutely!" said Auntie Meg firmly. "Tiger and I are going to have a ball together!"

"He'll certainly keep you busy," said Mum with a smile.

"He will but it'll be wonderful to have a kitten to love. Thanks so much for letting me adopt him, twins." Auntie Meg glanced at the window where Tiger was peering out. "Well now, I'd better be off."

"Bye, Meg," Mum said.

Auntie Meg hesitated and then suddenly stepped forward and hugged her. Mum looked surprised but very pleased.

Auntie Meg motioned to the twins. "Come on, you two."

Grace and Jack beamed and joined in.

"I'm really glad you're going to be Tiger's forever home," Grace told her aunt.

"Promise you'll come and see us again soon?" Jack said.

"Yes, promise," Grace insisted as they drew apart.

"I promise." Auntie Meg raised her eyebrows. "But are you asking because you want to see me or the kitten, or because of my cakes?"

 82

"Tiger and the cakes, of course!" said Grace with a cheeky grin. She squealed as her aunt tickled her. "Only joking!" she gasped. "We love you too."

Auntie Meg blinked and cleared her throat. "Right, well, I'd best be off!" she said briskly. She untied the *Happy Otter* and jumped back on board, but as she did so, Grace saw a smile pulling at her aunt's mouth.

The engine rumbled to life and Tiger came out of the cabin. He leapt on to the roof of the boat and stood between the flowerpots, his ears pricked, his tail up, watching them as he and Auntie Meg puttered away.

The twins waved until the *Happy Otter* was out of sight.

"Another happy ending," said Mum, putting her arm around their shoulders.

"Two happy endings hopefully," said Grace contentedly. "Tiger *and* Connie. Our very first double rehoming."

"Four happy endings if you count Auntie Meg and Barbara," added Jack.

Grace high-fived him. "And there are going to be lots more Forever Homes happy endings to come!" she declared.

AUNTIE MEG'S FACT FILE

NAME: Auntie Meg

AGE: Forty-six

LIKES: Cats, canal boats, cafes, visiting new places, colourful hair dye and BAKING!

DISLIKES: Staying in one place for too long

FAVOURITE COLOURS: Red, green and yellow

HOBBIES: Creating new recipes

FAVOURITE FOODS: Red velvet cake and bacon sandwiches

WHAT ANIMAL WOULD YOU BE?: A canal-boat cat lying on a sunny deck, watching the world drift by

HISS-TERICAL CAT JOKES!

WHY WAS THE CAT SITTING ON THE COMPUTER?

To keep an eye on the mouse!

WHAT DID THE CAT SAY WHEN THE MOUSE GOT AWAY?

You've got to be kitten me!

WHAT DO YOU CALL A PILE OF KITTENS?

A meowntain!

WHY WAS THE BIG CAT DISQUALIFIED FROM THE GAME?

Because it was a cheetah!

COOL KITTY
WORD JUMBLE

Are you a cool kitty or a mixed up Manx? Unscramble the words below to find the parts of a cat.

1. wap   **2.** lait

3. lawcs   **4.** skerwhis

5. toac   **6.** seon

ANSWERS ON PAGE 90

ANSWERS TO WORD JUMBLE ON PAGE 89

1. paw **2.** tail **3.** claws **4.** whiskers

5. coat **6.** nose

   90